It's five years since Ben Tennyson last transformed into aliens and fought crime with his cousin Gwen and their Grandpa Max.

Now 15 years old, Ben is once again forced to turn to the Omnitrix to help fight a new and more sinister threat – the HighBreed, DNAliens and the Forever Knights, who team up to take over the world.

The watch-like Omnitrix has re-programmed itself and has a complete set of ten, brand new alien choices for Ben to get to grips with. Helped by his cousin Gwen with her magical powers and Ben's former enemy, Kevin E. Levin, Ben is soon all set to go hero once again!

NOW READ ON . . .

EGMONT
We bring stories to life

This edition first published in Great Britain 2010
by Egmont UK Limited
239 Kensington High Street
London W8 6SA

Cartoon Network, the logo, Ben 10 ALIEN FORCE
and all related characters and elements are trademarks
of and © 2010 Cartoon Network

Adapted by Barry Hutchison

1 3 5 7 9 10 8 6 4 2

Printed and bound in Great Britain

All rights reserved. No part of this publication may be
reproduced, stored in a retrieval system, or transmitted, in any
form or by any means, electronic, mechanical, photocopying,
recording or otherwise, without the prior permission of the
publisher and copyright owner.

The Forest Stewardship Council (FSC) is an international,
non-governmental organisation dedicated to promoting
responsible management of the world's forests. FSC operates
a system of forest certification and product labelling that
allows consumers to identify wood and wood-based products
from well-managed forests.

For more information about Egmont's paper buying policy,
please visit www.egmont.co.uk/ethicalpublishing
For more information about the FSC, please visit their
website at www.fsc.org

ALL THAT GLITTERS

CHAPTER ONE

A MESSAGE FROM MAX

Lucy stood there in the near-darkness, her neat school uniform doing little to protect her from the cold evening air. Right before her was the thick, heavy door of a sprawling mansion.

'Let me in,' she pleaded, as her fists pounded against the varnished timber of the door. She could feel her hand beginning to bruise. 'I need to see you,' she begged, her arms sagging as her strength began to fade. 'Please.'

Lucy rested her head against the door. She was tired. So very tired. If she could just rest a moment then maybe she'd figure out some way to . . .

With a faint click the porch light flicked on, illuminating the girl on the step. An excited gasp slipped from her lips as she stepped back and raised her head. A lock was turned; a bolt was slid back. Lucy watched the door as it inched slowly open with a **CREEEEEAK**.

There was no light inside the house. As Lucy moved to step through the door something flashed in the dark. A round mouth ringed with rows of razor-sharp teeth lunged suddenly from the shadows, cutting off Lucy's scream before it even had a chance to start.

A short time later, not too far away, three teenagers discussed their plans for the evening. There was a school test coming up, and all three of them were worried.

'I'll meet you guys at the library after dinner,' suggested one boy. 'About – '

A sound from somewhere along the street stopped him in his tracks. All three teenagers listened. There it was again: a low moan that sent a shiver along their spines.

The sound of a shuffled footstep scuffing on the pavement made them jump. They came face to face with a young girl in school uniform.

Only the girl didn't look young at all. Her skin was grey, stretched tightly over her sunken cheekbones. Her body was frail and withered, and her dark eyes had not a trace of life in them.

The three friends turned and ran, screaming in terror, as the zombie that had been Lucy slowly shuffled off into the night.

Grandpa Max's face was blurred and a little distorted, but his voice was crystal clear. Ben sat on the kerb outside a corner shop, studying the tiny hologram of his grandfather. When the message ended he hit the button to play the recording again.

'If you've found this, you're in pretty deep,' Grandpa Max's hologram warned. 'There's a lot I can't reveal yet, but here's one thing I can. You can't go it alone.'

'By now you're probably meeting some of the other Plumbers' kids. But you have to find more. You need to put together a team.'

A few parking spaces away from Ben, Kevin was leaning on the bonnet of his car. Gwen, Ben's cousin, stood beside Kevin. Her arms were folded and she had a serious expression on her face. Kevin knew what that look meant. There was trouble ahead.

'Think we should be worried about him?' Kevin asked, nodding across to Ben, who had started to replay the recording again. 'He's been watching that thing for hours.'

Gwen didn't reply, but Kevin noticed her foot had begun to tap impatiently on the pavement. That was never a good sign.

'Problem?' he asked, trying to remember anything he might have done to upset her.

'Why haven't you asked me out?' Gwen suddenly demanded.

'What?' Kevin spluttered.

'You heard me. We spend all of our time together and you obviously like me.'

'Ha!' laughed Kevin, quickly turning his head away.

'You do,' Gwen insisted. 'I see you watching me when you think I'm not looking.'

Kevin opened his mouth to argue, but Gwen wasn't going to give him the chance.

'And I like you,' she smiled. 'Most of the time. So I'm asking you again – '

'See, that's the problem,' snapped Kevin. 'You're asking me. A guy does the asking.'

'Yeah?' asked Gwen with a smirk. 'When?'

'Don't push me,' Kevin said.

Gwen shook her head and sighed. She turned and stormed angrily away, leaving Kevin wishing he hadn't reacted the way he had. He knew he should call her back and say sorry, but after years as a villain, he still hadn't quite got the hang of being nice to people.

Instead he turned his attention to Ben, who was still sitting on the cold stone kerb, still watching the hologram of his grandfather repeating the same message for about the thousandth time.

'You know, my dog used to gnaw on this spot on his butt over and over,' Kevin announced. 'The vet made us put a cone around his neck.'

At first, Ben didn't reply. He was focused completely on the image of his Grandpa Max as the recording came to an end once more.

'Easy does it,' he told Kevin, getting up from the kerb. 'I'm not the one you're mad at.'

'Cut me a break here,' Kevin pleaded. He needed something to take his mind off his row with Gwen. 'You want to go fight some aliens or something?'

'Or something,' Ben nodded. 'Let me see your Plumber's badge.'

Kevin reached into his pocket, dug out the shiny green and black badge and tossed it to Ben. At the flick of a switch a detailed map was projected into the air just a few centimetres above the badge's surface. At various points around the map, several small white dots blinked on and off.

'Each of these blips shows the location of another badge,' Ben explained.

Kevin shrugged. 'Yep.'

'And where there's a Plumber's badge, we'll find a Plumber,' continued Ben. 'Or at least a Plumber's kid.'

The map vanished back down into the badge, as Ben passed the device back to Kevin.

'C'mon,' Ben urged, hurrying around to the passenger door of Kevin's car. 'We're off, and you're driving.'

Kevin took a step towards the driver's door, then paused. He turned and looked towards Gwen, who was leaning against a nearby lamp post, her back to the boys.

'You coming?' Kevin asked.

Gwen raised her head, scowled at him, then crossed to the car and climbed into the back without saying a word.

Kevin's car roared along the fast lane of a busy motorway, its powerful headlights slicing easily through the dark.

Up front, Ben was studying the blips on the glowing green map. In the back, Gwen was still in a bad mood.

'Plumber. Plumber. Plumber, Plumber, Plumber,' she sang. 'You ever notice that if you say a word enough times it loses its meaning?' Gwen stared at Kevin. 'Like a chance to ask someone out. Every time that chance comes along it has less and less meaning, until you don't have the chance any more at all.'

In the driver's seat, Kevin rolled his eyes. 'Oh,' he mumbled, 'for crying out loud.'

On another stretch of the motorway, less than half a mile ahead, a schoolgirl named Trina was shuffling along the side of the road. Her dark skin was wrinkle-free, and her limbs still looked strong, but from the way she was stumbling there was obviously something very wrong.

She staggered into the first lane of the motorway, her legs barely able to support her.

Trina didn't hear the blaring of the truck's horn. She didn't notice the squealing of brakes, or the cry of panic from the driver as he struggled to avoid smashing directly into her.

KAA-RAASH!

The truck toppled sideways as it turned, hitting the concrete hard. The vehicle's weight carried it onwards, metal screeching noisily as it scraped and sparked across the concrete.

BOOM!

With a sound like thunder, the truck crashed hard against the stone support pillar of the road bridge that crossed above this section of the motorway. The force of the crash shattered the pillar to dust. The sharp screams of terrified motorists split the night air, as the entire bridge began to crumble to pieces.

CHAPTER TWO

TEAMWORK IN ACTION

Kevin jammed his foot down hard on the brake, bringing the car to a halt less than a metre from a widening crack in the tarmac. They managed to stop just before the bridge, so they were safe. The same couldn't be said for the dozens of other cars that were slowly sliding towards the collapsing edge. It was a fifteen metre drop to the road below. No one inside those vehicles would survive the fall.

Ben, Gwen and Kevin leapt into action. In just a few seconds the whole bridge would collapse. There was no time to lose.

The man who had been driving the truck was stuck inside his cab. A fire had broken out and was spreading quickly along the length of the vehicle. The driver banged on the glass and shouted for help. As Kevin scrambled down the embankment to rescue him, Ben and Gwen turned their attention to the bridge itself.

One of the cars had begun sliding more quickly than the others. Ben gasped as he realised it was rolling right towards the side of the bridge. The whole structure was leaning sideways now, and there was nothing to stop the car plunging over the edge.

'Gwen!' Ben cried, but his cousin was already on to it. Twin beams of pink energy snaked from her hands. They streaked through the night, racing to get ahead of the sliding car.

Inside the vehicle, the driver and his family shut their eyes, holding on to each other tightly. They screamed as they felt the car tip, before realising they weren't falling nearly as quickly as they'd expected.

Opening his eyes, the driver peered outside. The car slid gently down a glowing slope of magical energy, before coming to a gentle rest in a safe area below.

A cloud of white dust billowed up from the bridge as more and more stone began to break away. Drivers and passengers swarmed from inside their cars, running frantically to try to get away.

KE-RRACK!

The concrete structure shook violently, sending a few of the runners stumbling towards the drop. Two more energy beams extended from Gwen's fingertips. They merged together, forming another long slope.

The fleeing people flashed Gwen a grateful smile as they leapt one-by-one on to the slide and slipped down to the safety of the ground below.

There were too many of them, Ben knew. Too many people, and not enough time before the bridge gave way completely. There was no way they would all make it, unless . . .

Ben twisted the dial of the Omnitrix and the hologram of a hulking, dinosaur-like alien flashed up. With a slam he activated the alien watch, and a cloud of green energy swirled around him.

Ben felt his heart swell in his chest and his bones begin to grow. His skin stretched and grew thicker, as a row of spiky plates extended from his spine and the muscular tail that sprouted from beneath it.

In less than a second, Ben was gone. In his place stood the hulking Humungousaur!

The dinosaur alien bounded over the side of the bridge, his powerful feet cracking the concrete where he landed. The collapsing structure was several metres above him. Fortunately, that wasn't a problem.

All around the motorway, onlookers pointed and stared, as Humungousaur's already giant frame began to expand. Up and up he stretched, until his mighty shoulders were wedged tightly against the underside of the bridge.

The alien gritted his sharp teeth. The weight of the bridge with all those cars on top was almost unbearable. Even with his incredible strength, he wouldn't be able to support it for long.

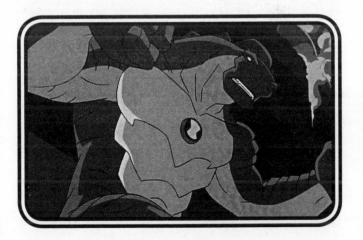

'Get everyone down,' he barked at Gwen. 'I can't hold this together much longer.'

Gwen was working as fast as she could, but there were at least twenty people still waiting to slide to safety. She glanced nervously down at the road below. Kevin was there, pulling the truck driver free from his burning cab. Another life saved. Only the people on the bridge were in danger now.

And then Gwen saw her – the shambling shape of Trina, still wandering aimlessly across the road. A car was speeding towards her, the driver too distracted by the events on the bridge to see what was directly in his path.

'The girl!' Gwen cried.

Kevin looked up and spotted Trina. He was too far away. He couldn't reach her in time. 'Ben!' he bellowed, desperately.

Humungousaur could see what was happening, but if he moved from the bridge it would surely collapse, killing all those still

stranded on it. 'Hands . . . full,' he managed
to growl.

At last the driver of the car saw Trina
standing in front of him, but he was too late.
She was too close by the time he spotted her.
There was no way he could avoid knocking
her down.

Suddenly, a streak of yellow light tore
down from the sky. The strong arms of a
glowing, golden figure wrapped around Trina's
waist, before they both launched skywards, out
of the path of the speeding car.

Gwen watched the scene unfold, her eyes wide with wonder. She was so fixed on the shimmering outline of Trina's rescuer that she barely noticed the last few people had already slid down to safety.

'Everyone's OK,' she announced, finally. The power-beam escape slide fizzled out, and Gwen floated down to join Kevin.

With a grunt, Humungousaur let the bridge go. It collapsed instantly, sending huge chunks of shattered stone raining down on the now empty truck.

One quick flash of green later, and the enormous alien became the considerably less gigantic Ben. He rushed over to join Gwen and Kevin, and all three of them watched the mysterious hero drift back to Earth, still carrying Trina in his arms.

As his feet touched the ground, the golden outline faded, revealing a blonde-haired, blue-eyed boy of around Ben's age. He had a square jaw and was smartly dressed, like a lead actor in an old adventure movie.

Trina jolted awake as he sat her on the pavement. 'I – I have to get out of here,' she wailed. 'I was running, and I . . . I . . .'

'It's OK, Trina,' the boy assured her. 'You're safe now.'

A whimper escaped Trina's lips, but she seemed to relax a little. Her rescuer looked up at

Ben, Gwen and Kevin who stood next to him.

'Whoever you guys are, whatever you are, thanks,' he said. His eyes flicked back to Trina. 'Something strange has been happening to the girls at our school lately.'

'Glad to help. We made a good team out there,' replied Ben, before a familiar green and black logo on the boy's belt caught his eye. 'You've got a Plumber's badge,' he gasped.

'Yeah, my dad gave it to me,' said the blonde-haired boy. 'You guys know about the Plumbers?'

Kevin pulled his own badge from his pocket and held it up. 'At this point, we may as well be them.'

'I'm Ben Tennyson. This is Kevin and my cousin, Gwen.'

The boy's eyes grew wide. 'Wait. Ben Tennyson?' he asked. 'I'm a huge fan of yours. But I heard you disappeared.' He stood up and took hold of Ben's hand, shaking it firmly. 'My name is Mike Morningstar.'

Morningstar shook Kevin's hand, too, before moving on to Gwen. As their hands touched, a spark of yellow electricity fizzled between their palms.

'Oh!' Gwen gasped.

'Wow,' said Morningstar. 'That's never happened before.'

'Maybe it's because we both have powers,' suggested Gwen.

Morningstar smiled. 'That's a theory.'

'Anyway,' coughed Kevin, stepping between the pair, 'now that we've all met?'

Morningstar managed to tear his eyes away from Gwen's.

'I should make sure Trina gets home OK,' Morningstar announced. 'But after that, why don't we meet up at my place and talk?'

'Sure,' said Ben.

'Sounds good,' agreed Gwen.

Kevin groaned. 'Can't wait.'

With a final nod, Morningstar scooped Trina up in his arms and leapt up into the sky. The golden glow surrounded him in an instant, covering him, Trina, and the circle-shaped marking that appeared to be burned on to Trina's forearm.

A marking that looked a lot like a round mouth full of very sharp teeth.

CHAPTER THREE

A ZOMBIE PLAGUE

orningstar's 'place' turned out to be a plush apartment in the grounds of his family's stately home. The expensive carpet padded softly beneath their feet as Ben, Gwen and Kevin followed Morningstar inside.

'Mum and her new husband live in the main house,' Morningstar explained. 'They leave me alone. Let me do what I want.'

'Cool,' whistled Ben.

Morningstar opened the door and stepped back, motioning for Gwen to go through. 'After you,' he smiled.

Gwen gave Kevin a brief smirk, then stepped through the doorway. Ben followed, with Morningstar a step behind. Before Kevin could follow them, the door swung shut on his face with a hard slam.

Kevin pushed open the door and stormed through, rubbing his nose where the door had hit it, and muttering below his breath. 'Nice.'

The room they had entered was bigger than Ben's whole house. Banks of computers and other high-tech gadgets covered almost every surface. Tiny lights blinked and flashed on them, like a thousand distant stars.

'What is all this stuff?' asked Ben.

'Some of my dad's Plumber gear. I brought it over from his headquarters.' Morningstar turned to Gwen. 'I could take you there later if you want.'

'We'd all like to see it,' enthused Ben.

'It'd make my day for sure,' Kevin scowled, sarcastically.

Morningstar's gaze was still fixed on Gwen. 'Here,' he said, taking her by the hand, 'let me show you something.'

They walked across to where a giant

monitor covered a large section of wall. On the screen was a series of complicated-looking maps, diagrams and symbols.

'I'm patched into the central Plumbers' monitoring network,' Morningstar explained. 'It's connected to everything. Global and interplanetary internet. Earthbound law enforcement frequencies. Oh, and of course the badge communicator channel.'

Kevin and Ben glanced at each other, then down at Kevin's badge. 'Communicator channel?' Kevin asked.

Morningstar raised one eyebrow. 'Yeah. You did know the badges are communicators, didn't you?'

'So,' said Gwen, before the boys could admit they didn't, 'you keep an eye on things with this stuff and use your powers to help people. You're like your neighbourhood's very own superhero.'

'Never thought of it that way,'

Morningstar replied, 'but I guess so.'

Ben had been watching the boy closely, and he was impressed by what he saw. He nodded as he came to a decision.

'You know that I'm thinking?' he said.

'I know what I'm thinking,' mumbled Kevin, too quietly for anyone to hear.

'You should come and join our team,' suggested Ben.

'Don't you think we should, I don't know, get to know this guy a little more?' asked Kevin.

'What's to know? He's got the powers, he's got the gear. And it's what Grandpa told us to do.'

Kevin began to protest, but Ben stepped away and continued talking to Morningstar. 'My Grandpa Max was a Plumber, and he disappeared while looking into this big alien conspiracy that's going on against Earth. We're trying to find him so we can stop it. Do you want to help us?'

Morningstar's eyes flicked across to Gwen. 'I'd love to,' he said with a smile.

Without warning, the lights in the apartment began to flicker and dim. Some of the computer monitors went dark, but the main terminal managed to remain on.

Then, as suddenly as it had started, the electricity problem stopped, and full power was restored to the room.

'Perhaps you forgot to pay your electric bill?' sneered Kevin.

'The electricity's been a little unreliable lately. No worries, my backup generator has kicked in.'

'This isn't a black-out,' said Ben. He was staring up at the big computer screen. 'Look at this spike in power usage at the local power substation. The energy drain is enormous.'

'Really?' frowned Morningstar.

'You said that something strange was happening in town,' Ben continued.

'And this definitely qualifies.'

'If you need to check it out, we'll help,' volunteered Gwen.

'Thanks,' Morningstar nodded. 'Well, perhaps we should go to the substation now.'

All four of them made for the door, Morningstar leading the way. Halfway to the exit, something on her wrist caught Gwen's eye. A quiet cry of shock caught in her throat as she looked down and realised a strange, circular pattern had begun to form on her skin, just like the one she'd noticed on Trina's.

She pulled her sleeve lower, covering up the mark. She could worry about it later. Right now, there was a mystery to solve.

The low, squat buildings of the electrical substation were in near-darkness when Ben and the others approached the gate. A steady high-voltage hum was the only indication that the station was even up and running.

A padlock and chain lay on the ground beside the fence. Ben nudged the gate and it swung open without a sound.

'Stay sharp,' Ben whispered, sneaking through the open gate. 'We've got company.'

The electrical hum seemed to grow louder and louder as the group crept stealthily across the grounds of the substation. Morningstar glanced up at one of the tall pylons that loomed high overhead.

'Sounds like that weird buzzing sound you always hear in old monster movies,' he whispered.

Ben gulped, stopped abruptly and pointed ahead. Before them, the withered, zombie-like outline of a girl stood between two pylons, her bony arms stretched above her. Tendrils of electricity crackled from the metal posts.

They wrapped around the girl. Her eyes glowed an eerie shade of white as she absorbed the energy into her body.

With a sudden start, the girl realised she was being watched. She ducked sideways and tore a large piece of machinery from the base of the pylon, lifting it easily over her head.

With a hiss of animal rage, the zombie girl hurled the machinery towards the group. Gwen threw up her hands. A shield of magical energy surrounded them, deflecting the projectile at the last second.

With a low moan, another girl shambled from the shadows beside them. Her frail arms were outstretched, her lifeless eyes staring blankly. Another girl emerged behind her, then another, and another, until the heroes found themselves facing an entire horde of zombies.

'The girls here?' said Ben, nervously. 'Kinda weird.'

'They're wearing uniforms from my school,' Morningstar said. 'But I don't recognise any of them.'

One of the zombies ripped a metal post clean out of the ground. She advanced again,

swinging the steel pole like a baseball bat.

Stepping protectively in front of Gwen, Morningstar raised his clenched fists. Twin bands of golden power exploded from them. The beams struck the ground in front of the approaching zombies, forcing them backwards a few paces.

'Energy bolts,' cried Ben. 'Nice.'

'Try not to hurt them,' Morningstar urged. 'Maybe we can reverse this. Whatever it is.'

'Try not to hurt them?' snorted Kevin, as the pole-wielding zombie lunged at him, snarling angrily. He ducked the clumsy swing and rolled sideways to where another post jutted up from the ground.

Pressing his fingers against the metal, Kevin began to absorb its properties. His body took on the strength and appearance of polished steel. If these ladies wanted a fight, then he would be only too happy to give them one.

Ben stumbled backwards, struggling against the choke-hold of another zombie girl. His back slammed hard against a thick metal cabinet marked 'High Voltage' and he yelped with pain.

The girl released her grip, but quickly swung with a wild punch. Ben twisted to the side, barely avoiding the blow. He watched, amazed, as the girl's tiny fist drove a hole straight through the metal door.

The zombie screeched with inhuman rage as she pulled her hand free. The entire door tore away, and Ben realised the girl was now holding on to a thick electrical wire. Blue sparks, like mini lightning bolts, fizzled at the damaged end of the cable.

The girl began to advance once more, stabbing at him with the crackling cable. If it touched him he was done for. There was nothing else for it. Ben slammed the control dial of the Omnitrix.

It was hero time.

CHAPTER FOUR

A DESPERATE BATTLE

CLANG! The metal pole bounced harmlessly off Kevin's steel body. Moving quickly, Kevin threw a punch, lifting the girl off her feet, then dropping her to the ground. It should have been more than enough to knock her out, but somehow the girl got back up.

A flash of green caught his attention. Kevin glanced across to where Ben had been. A tall, purple and blue figure stood there, facing off against another of the zombies. Ben had transformed into the rock-bodied, crystal-formed ChromaStone.

With a roar, the zombie girl threw herself at the alien, jabbing the electrical cable into his chest. A lightning storm seemed to whip up around ChromaStone, buzzing and zapping across his stony surface.

'That's not going to work,' ChromaStone grinned. 'I'm a conductor.'

He extended a finger and pressed it against the girl's head. The electrical current passed harmlessly through his body and flowed into hers. As soon as the bright blue sparks touched her, the zombie screamed and toppled backwards on to the ground.

ChromaStone smiled, lifted his finger, and blew away the thin line of grey smoke that curled up from the tip.

A series of bright yellow streaks screamed down from above, striking the ground and throwing rock and debris in all directions. Morningstar was airborne, blasting at the ground, doing everything he could to drive the zombies back without hurting them.

Gwen's fingers danced, sending tendrils of pink energy snaking towards a few of the zombie girls. Like ropes, the energy trails wrapped around the girls, tying them tightly together. They struggled against their bonds, but Gwen was too strong.

Or was she?

A flicker of pain flitted across Gwen's face as the effort of using her powers suddenly became too much. The pink bands that held the zombies in place faded to black, before shattering like brittle glass.

Suddenly the world was spinning and Gwen was falling, too weak to even stand. A split second before her head hit the ground, a familiar golden figure caught her.

'Are you all right?' Morningstar asked.

'I . . . I don't know. I felt weak for a second,' Gwen stammered, struggling back upright. She looked up at Morningstar and smiled. 'I feel better now.'

Morningstar returned her smile. 'Here, hold my hand,' he said. 'Use my energy.'

The moment their hands met, Morningstar's glittering golden glow began to surround Gwen. His power recharged her, allowing her to project an energy shield and drive the approaching zombies back.

With the girls pushed back, Morningstar unleashed some power bolts at a nearby pylon. The tall metal structure folded in on itself like a house of cards. It crashed to the ground, forming a barrier between the zombies and the heroes.

Realising there was no possible way through, the zombie girls growled angrily, then turned and fled back into the shadows from where they came.

'Ah, nice going,' snapped Kevin, returning to his normal form. 'They are all getting away!'

'Sorry,' said Morningstar.

With a flurry of green energy, ChromaStone transformed back into Ben. He rested a hand on Morningstar's shoulder.

'It's OK. We all make mistakes,' he said, reassuringly. 'The important thing is we stopped them from . . . Uh, doing whatever it is they were doing. We'll get better as we work together more.'

Morningstar turned and stared deeply into Gwen's eyes. 'We do make a good team,' he smiled.

Gwen blushed slightly. 'Uh-huh.'

'What happened just now?' Kevin asked Gwen, trying to interrupt. 'You looked like you were gonna faint.'

Ignoring Kevin, Gwen smiled shyly up at Morningstar. 'I can't thank you enough for helping me.'

'You could if you had dinner with me.'

'Right now?' Gwen asked.

'I'm hungry. How about you?'

Gwen wrapped her arm around Morningstar's. 'I was just going to suggest the same thing.'

'OK, what is up with you?' Kevin demanded. 'You've been ignoring me ever since we got here, you were lousy in the fight and now you're just acting goofy.'

'Why are you pretending to care?' Gwen sneered, as she and Morningstar began to walk away. 'Later.'

Kevin watched them go, barely able to contain his anger. He spun to face Ben. 'You just gonna stand there?'

'No,' Ben replied. 'I was going to go sit in the car.'

'I don't trust this guy,' said Kevin, following Ben towards the car park. 'And I don't think you should have been so quick to make him one of the team.'

'Admit it, you're just jealous because

Gwen likes him.'

Kevin opened his mouth to argue, before an idea suddenly struck him.

'You know what?' he said with a sly grin. 'It's fine.'

One fast car journey later, and Ben and Kevin were standing outside the door of Morningstar's apartment. Kevin had used his absorbing abilities to turn his fingers to metal, and now had one jammed into the door's heavy lock. He wiggled the finger around inside the keyhole, listening for a click.

'This is why you changed your mind about Mike going off with Gwen?' Ben sighed. 'So we could spy on him?'

'Yeah,' Kevin smirked.

'Well, stop!'

'He ain't right, Ben,' Kevin insisted. 'If you're not gonna check him out, I am.'

'You're doing the wrong thing, Kevin. The old Kevin thing. Step away from the door.'

'You really want to fight me over some new guy?' Kevin asked. 'That's how you're gonna build a team?'

The lock mechanism gave a faint click and Kevin edged the door open. He smiled, pleased at himself. 'And they said I didn't learn anything in the Null Void.'

Before Kevin could step inside, both boys heard a familiar voice.

'Is Mike home?' asked Trina. She was shuffling up the path, her whole body shaking. 'He hasn't called me back since you and that new girl showed up.'

'Trina, right? Yeah, Morningstar ain't here right now,' Kevin replied. He realised she was looking at the open door. He had to think fast. 'We're . . . just picking up some stuff for him.'

'Then you know where he is!' Trina cried. 'Can you take me?'

'No,' said Ben. 'I mean, he's busy.'

Trina let out a soft sob of despair. 'I need to see him. Why won't he see me?'

Kevin studied the girl. She looked frail and weak – even worse than she'd looked at the motorway. His eyes fell to her trembling arms and he realised they were covered in dark, circular tattoos.

'Where'd you get those marks on your arms?' he asked. When the girl didn't answer, Kevin turned to Ben. 'I saw those same marks on that zombie girl that tried to tenderise me.'

'I just wanna see Mike,' Trina wept.

'Yeah, I'm getting that,' Kevin nodded. 'Call me crazy,' he told Ben, 'but do you think it's possible that Morningstar's the one making the girls this way?'

Ben blinked. 'You're crazy.'

'Look, it didn't really hit me 'til just now,'

Kevin continued, 'but I've noticed that Gwen's been wearing her sleeves lower than usual. She's hiding something.'

'You're saying Gwen has marks like that on her arms?'

'I haven't seen them for sure,' admitted Kevin, 'but it makes sense.'

Ben rubbed his chin, thoughtfully. 'Come to think of it, Trina was all weak and wobbly when we first saw her on the motorway. Gwen was the same way at the power plant. It's possible that Gwen might have caught whatever bug is doing this.'

'Yeah,' said Kevin, his eyes narrowing to slits. 'And the bug's name is Mike Morningstar.'

CHAPTER FIVE

THE FINAL CONFRONTATION

Smoke billowed from the tyres of Kevin's car as it screeched around a sharp bend in the road. Inside, Kevin pushed the accelerator pedal to the floor, powering the vehicle through the turn.

'Fact is you've been against Morningstar since the minute we met him,' Ben said. 'Because Gwen likes him more than she likes you.'

'Yeah, some of that,' Kevin said with a shrug. 'But now Gwen's in trouble, and you're too stuck on following your Grandpa's instructions to see it.'

Kevin spun the car around yet another corner, bouncing Ben around in the front passenger seat.

'Well, if Mike's turning those girls into creatures, why isn't Trina one?' Ben asked.

'I don't know. Maybe it's like a vampire thing. Maybe it takes a while before they go all zombie.'

'Even if you're right, we don't know where they went for dinner,' Ben pointed out. 'How are we supposed to find her?'

'Easy,' grinned Kevin, pulling out his Plumber's badge and activating the holo-map. 'We find him.'

Inside the abandoned bunker that had once been his father's secret headquarters, Morningstar was gripping Gwen tightly by her arms. Gwen looked barely conscious. Her skin was turning grey and wrinkled, as the life force was sucked out of her by the strange round

mouths that had appeared in the middle of
Morningstar's palms.

'Your energy is like nothing I've ever felt
before. When it flows into me, I feel invincible!'
Morningstar licked his lips, enjoying the taste of
the power. 'From the moment I touched you,
I knew I'd found the only girl I'd ever need.'

With a splintering of wood, the front door
of the building exploded inwards and Kevin and
Ben charged through. They stared in horror and
shock as they realised Kevin's suspicions had
been right all along.

'Gwen!' Kevin cried. He and Ben sprinted forwards, but a blast of yellow energy scorched the air around them. One of the bolts suddenly slammed into Ben's chest, sending him tumbling backwards.

Pressing his hands against the concrete floor, Kevin absorbed its strength. His body now rock-solid, he resumed his charge towards Morningstar and the helpless Gwen. 'Get away from her,' he roared.

Another sudden and powerful blast slammed into Kevin. Even in rock form he wasn't strong enough to deflect it. In a cloud of stone-dust he thudded hard against the back wall of the bunker.

Still dazed, Ben struggled to activate the Omnitrix. Gwen was lying on the floor now, barely moving. She didn't have much time left.

At last, Ben's fingers found the control dial. He pressed it down and sighed with relief, as the familiar swirl of green energy wrapped around him.

'Jet Ray!' he cried, launching his now bright-red alien form into the air. Jet Ray's mighty wings flapped twice, circling him around to face his target. The alien unleashed the full fury of his neuroshock laser blasts on Morningstar, but they had no effect.

'Go away!' Morningstar roared. He fired a devastating energy-bolt that struck the flying alien hard. With a groan, Jet Ray plunged to the ground. By the time he struck the concrete, he had already turned back into Ben.

Morningstar's eyes blazed. 'Gwen's mine now.'

Kevin had something to say about that. He sprinted forwards and hurled himself at the glowing figure, knocking him to the floor. A concrete fist slammed into Morningstar's jaw and he hissed in pain.
Before Kevin could land another punch, a blast of yellow light sent him backflipping off the fallen villain. The blow was so powerful it shattered the stone shell surrounding Kevin, stripping it away and turning him back into

flesh and bone.

'You're out of your league,' Morningstar sneered. 'All I ever wanted was power and then you brought me Gwen.'

Ben tried to get to his feet, but he hadn't recovered from Morningstar's blast. From the shadows he spotted the shuffling shapes of the zombie girls they'd fought at the power station. They were advancing slowly, shambling towards the fallen heroes.

'I guess I should thank you,' Morningstar said. His eyes flicked up to the ceiling, where a huge air-conditioning pipe hung above Ben and Kevin. The villain smiled and raised his hands. 'I know the perfect thing.'

Still grinning, Morningstar unleashed a power bolt. It screamed through the air, on a direct collision course with the heavy length of metal pipe.

Just before it brought the whole thing crashing down, the energy blast fizzled and faded. Morningstar frowned, then looked down to where a withered hand was clutching one of his feet.

It took all her remaining strength, but Gwen pulled herself up. She held Morningstar's arms, and the air around her shimmered as she began to take her life force back.

'What are you doing?' Morningstar cried.

'Coming to my senses,' Gwen replied. The energy flowed into her, faster and faster. In seconds her withered frame was back to normal, her skin no longer grey.

'Stop this!' pleaded Morningstar, but it was too late. He screamed as the last of the energy he had stolen from Gwen left his body. Gwen released her grip, leaving Morningstar to slump to the floor.

'Kevin!' she cried, running over to where the two boys were still lying.

'Girls,' barked Morningstar, motioning to the zombies. 'Come here to me.'

Moaning softly, the girls turned and shuffled towards the energy thief. 'Give me your power,' he ordered them. 'Help me. Feed me.'

The girls shuffled closer. There would be feeding done, but Morningstar wouldn't be the one to do it. He screamed once again as the zombie girls all took hold of him, sucking their energy back into their withered bones.

In a few moments it was all over. Gasping for breath, Morningstar lay motionless on the floor. Around him, the girls who had been his victims sneered down in disgust. They were back to normal now, and they would never fall for his tricks again.

Kevin reached down and plucked the Plumber's badge from Morningstar's belt. 'You don't deserve this,' he said.

And with that, Kevin crushed the badge into dust.

Kevin drove them away from the bunker.

'I'm sorry I took Morningstar's side over yours,' Ben said to Kevin. He turned to Gwen. 'And that I wasn't watching your back.'

'It wasn't your fault,' Gwen replied. 'Morningstar had some kind of control over me.'

'It was my fault,' Ben insisted. 'I was in such a hurry to build our team, I ignored the danger. If I'm going to be a good leader, I'm going to need to show better judgement.'

'If you're gonna be a good leader, you need to stop sounding like such a fool,' Kevin suggested.

A wicked smile spread across Ben's face. 'So Kevin,' he asked. 'When are you gonna ask Gwen out?'

Oh great, thought Kevin. Here we go again!